BOBINA
AT
NEVADIER

- A Short Story Series -

CHARLES MWEWA

DEDICATION

For

Emmerance

CONTENTS

ABOUT THE STORY

Bobina Cavmozt, a native of the Kronozo Planet, wakes up on another planet, Nevadier, and discovers that he has been adopted as the next heir to Auntie Coparavia's empire. Coparavia is the reigning Grand Beloved of the Nevadierenes. Bobina, a convict and forsaken of the Kronozoes, is now a celebrated chosen first citizen of the Nevadierenes. He must quickly come to terms as a new philosophy in government, the *Grace Charter*, endorsed by the Council of Nevadier at the Palace of Mirrors, the first of its kind in Govius Universe, takes effect.

BOBINA AT NEVADIER

Bobina woke up from a long, restful night.

"Copa, is breakfast ready?"

"Yes, it is. Let me know if there's anything I should do for you."

It had been nearly a month since Bobina was teleported and inadvertently landed at the western shores of Nevadier, near the Palace of Mirrors.

Bobina remembered how it all happened.

Bobina was from a neighboring planet called Kronozo. Like all other seventeen planets in the Govius Universe, rules dictated the order of life.

Bobina worked as a craftsman at an antique store called Muirand Curios. One Friday evening, he mistakenly left the shop unlocked because he had a prearranged dinner with his fiancée, Jemrora. While dining with Jemrora, he remembered that he might have left the shop unlocked.

"I must be going, Jem, I think I forgot to lock the shop?"

"No, don't go, Bob, you understand that I have been waiting for this dinner for months."

"B-but…"

Bobina was intercepted and stopped from going. Jemrora had threatened that if he did go, she would break off the engagement.

Just then Jemrora received a call.

"Hold on, I need this one, if you don't mind?"

"Of course, I don't," Bobina reassured.

Jemrora left and entered in the female washroom to answer the call.

"*Of course, Grekk, you may proceed,*" Jemrora whispered.

"*Roger that,*" Grekk whispered back.

Jemrora returned to the table, where she had left Bobina. She looked a bit absent-minded.

Bobina took it that his fiancée was equally rattled by the likelihood that he might have left the shop unlocked or that she didn't want him to postpone the dinner.

"Alright, hope something awful doesn't happen. There is a money safe in there," Bobina said.

"Don't worry, Darling, no-one knows that you didn't lock," Jemrora convinced Bobina.

Someone sitting near the couple's table had heard them. But they didn't seem to care.

*****

"Bobina was the last person to leave the shop yesterday, and there is no evidence of forced entry," reported Mumboo, the General Manager of Muirand Curios, to the police constable who was investigating the theft of 400 *Krozods*, an equivalent of \$11.2 million, inside the safe.

The safe was uprooted from its source and taken together with the money inside it.

The management of Muirand Curios pressed robbery charges against Bobina.

At trial, Bobina's only *alibi* witness was his fiancée, Jemrora. However, Jemrora could not devour the information that she was the one who advised him against returning to lock up the shop.

Bobina *loved* Jemrora.

*****

Bobina lost the case and was convicted of robbery.

He was sentenced to life imprisonment at the Pendago Penitentiary, a mining prison on the conquered Pendago Planet.

Later, his sentence was upgraded to banishment. Bobina had no idea why his sentence was upgraded. When he consulted a lawyer in prison, she advised him that there was a rarely used declaration under penalty of perjury in the *Penal Code* that if an informant swore an oath that further implicated the convict, after sentence, the "dangerous offender" sentence might be invoked to upgrade the sentence.

"Or…" the lawyer began, "Anyone who steals any amount more than three-hundred and ninety-nine *Krozods* is to be banished and subjected to hard labor until they die. This last amendment to the *Penal Code* came into effect sometimes last year."

Bobina could not appeal the sentence because he had already missed the limitation period of thirty-days. And before Bobina could say bye-bye to his guilty-laden fiancée, he was on the teleporter to Pendago.

The only escape at Pendago Penitentiary was usually death.

*****

When Bobina opened his eyes, he did not find himself at Pendago, but around the western shores of Nevadier.

"I must be dreaming…" he tried to remember, "How did I find myself here?" he questioned.

There and then, he saw two graceful Nevadierenes looking at him, grinning nonchalantly.

They're just like us, the Kronozoes, Bobina begins thinking. *But they must be an inch taller than us, on average, I think. They're a bit darker in complexion than us.*

"Welcome home, my name is Xiera," the first one of the Nevadierenes saluted and introduced himself.

"My name is Vzer, and I am with Xiera."

"What's your name?" Xiera asked.

"They call me Bob; my real name is Bobina. Bobina Cavmozt," he answered.

"Nice to meet you, Bob," Vzer reached out.

5

"We must be going. Auntie Coparavia is waiting to receive you at the Palace of Mirrors," said Xiera.

Who is Auntie Coparavia, what is the Palace of Mirrors, Bobina thought.

As the trio was driving off in the *Dux* – an AI-minted airvehicle – Xiera explained that their cadets on reconnaissance had spotted the wreckage of the Pendago teleporter, the *Star of Pendago*, along the shores. All the seventeen others on board had perished except Bobina.

After about fifteen minutes, they arrived at the magnificent Palace of Mirrors to a hero's welcome. There was a pageantry of boys and girls dressed in rainbow attires with musical instruments Bobina had never seen before. Everyone stood in offhand positions, without rank or seniority.

Everyone looked the same to Bobina.

This is strange here, Bobina thinks. *There is no rank or chivalry here as they do at Kronozo. I don't even know who the most important of them is in this crowd.*

Just then, a red carpet rolled, and to Bobina's surprise, it was rolled for him.

*****

"That was delicious, Ma'am…" Bobina stopped himself in midsentence. He remembered how his "30-day-orientation" to Nevadierene life had been programed.

He was there. He had attended. In fact, he was the subject of the last First Council of Nevadier. At the Council, they had voted overwhelmingly for him to be under the care of the 11th Councilor, Mobim Kojko. But Auntie Coparavia had used her veto power to overrule.

"Bob will be under my care. As you know, I've been his *de facto* concierge since he arrived at Nevadier," she had said.

Everyone in the Council stood up to an ovation and erupted in chants of:

"*Grace Charter!*
Grace Charter!
Grace Charter!"

Bobina turned towards Kembololo, whom they had made acquaintances for the month he had spent at the Palace of Mirrors, and asked:

"Why are they chanting *Grace Charter*?"

Kembo, as they shortened his name, whispered back into Bobina's ear, "It's the new thing at Nevadier; the leader and the subject are considered equals."

It explains why Ma'am has been serving me all this time, Bobina thought.

When the chant had subsided, Auntie Coparavia continued her speech:

"Dearly beloved,

I must overrule your most gracious vote and offer myself as Bob's caretaker."

The Council had nodded.

Councilor Kojko stood up and gestured to the Council that he wanted to speak. Beloved Speaker, Jobdom Pedko, sustained.

"For the record, 11th Councilor, Speaker. I respectfully surrender the guardianship of Bobina to the Grand Beloved. May her will be done."

Kojko sat.

Then the 3rd Councilor beckoned to the Speaker to speak, and for her, it was also sustained.

"For the record, Zzeb Kenadb, 3rd Councilor. You've clearly outdone us all in the virtue of kindness, Grand Beloved. May your will be done."

Kenadb sat.

Without adhering to protocol, he stood up, and started talking as he simultaneously beckoned to the Speaker's bench for attention.

"For three suns and four moons, I've spent time searching for someone I should show and share kindness with, and, alas, to no avail. Comrades, I have been almost tempted to leave this planet and seek for someone out of Nevadier."

The entire assembly erupted in laughter.

"It's me, the 8th Councilor, Mijid Judo, for the record, Speaker."

And Judo sat.

"What kind of people are these, Bobina thought. *They even compete to outdo each other in altruism. I should have figured it out why Ma'am has been treating me, as if I was the president, and she was my assistant."*

At the closing of the meeting, Coparavia and Bobina left together.

"After you, Bob," Coparavia offered.

"I should follow after you, Grand Beloved, Ma'am."

Coparavia stepped ahead of Bobina. She held his right arm tightly and gently whispered in his ears.

"Copa, call me Copa."

*****

"How was breakfast?" Coparavia asked.

"Amazing, like always – like it has been in the last more than a month since I arrived here," Bobina was excited.

Coparavia gathered all utensils and cutlery Bobina had just used. She carefully loaded the dishwasher and at the same time she made a gesture to Bobina as if telling him that, "I have already prepared your study."

Bobina nodded with a sigh of gratitude and then said, "Thanks, Copa."

"That's more like it, *Copa*, indeed, it is," Coparavia expressed her deep appreciation for being addressed informally.

What am I supposed to do today? I did finish reviewing the Charter, *but I still have some questions for Copa*, Bobina thought.

Coparavia sensed that Bobina had some unanswered questions by observing his demeanor.

"Is anything the matter, Bob?"

Before Bobina could utter a word, Coparavia approached him, caressed his right arm gingerly and waited for him to respond.

Bobina could not find a more suitable word

to use to thank the mother of the entire planet treating him with such courtesy and endearment that not even Jemrora could compare.

All these are just for a convict like me. What did I do to deserve such A-plus treatment from the matriarchy herself, Bobina pondered.

Sensing that Bobina was too quiet, Coparavia repeated her question, "Anything the matter?"

"Nothing, Copa. I wanted to say…"

"That you finished reading the *Charter*?"

"How did you know what I was going to say, Copa?"

"I didn't. Just a calculated guess, a hunch, I suppose."

"Well, I think I've begun to understand."

"To understand what, Bob?"

"That concept contained in that *Charter*."

"You mean 'grace'?" Coparavia probed.

"I think so," Bobina said.

[*READ THE NEXT EPISODE*]

ABOUT THE AUTHOR

Best Selling Author, Charles Mwewa (LLB; BA Law; BA Ed; LLM), is a prolific researcher, poet, novelist, lawyer, law professor and Christian apologist and intercessor. Mwewa has written no less than 73 books and counting in every genre and has exhibited his works at prestigious expos like the Ottawa International Book Expo and is the winner of the Coppa Awards for his signature publication, *Zambia: Struggles of My People.*

SELECTED BOOKS BY THIS AUTHOR

1. *ZAMBIA: Struggles of My People (First and Second Editions)*
2. *10 FINANCIAL & WEALTH ATTITUDES TO AVOID*
3. *10 STRATEGIES TO DEFEAT STRESS AND DEPRESSION: Creating an Internal Safeguard against Stress and Depression*
4. *100+ REASONS TO READ BOOKS*
5. *A CASE FOR AFRICA?S LIBERTY: The Synergistic Transformation of Africa and the West into First-World Partnerships*
6. *A PANDEMIC POETRY, COVID-19*
7. *ALLERGIC TO CORRUPTION: The Legacy of President Michael Sata of Zambia*
8. *BOOK ABOUT SOMETHING: On Ultimate Purpose*
9. *CAMPAIGN FOR AFRICA: A Provocative Crusade for the Economic and Humanitarian Decolonization of Africa*
10. *CHAMPIONS: Application of Common Sense and Biblical Motifs to Succeed in Both Worlds*
11. *CORONAVIRUS PRAYERS*
12. *HH IS THE RIGHT MAN FOR ZAMBIA: And Other Acclaimed Articles on Zambia and Africa*
13. *I BOW: 3500 Prayer Lines of Inspiration & Intercession from the Heart: Volume One*
14. *INTERUNIVERSALISM IN A NUTSHELL: For Iranian Refugee Claimants*
15. *LAW & GRACE: An Expository Study in the Rudiments of Sin and Truth*
16. *LAWS OF INFLUENCE: 7even Lessons in Transformational Leadership*